MOONBEAM

AND SUNNY

SELMA AND JACK
WASSERMANN

ILLUSTRATIONS
GEORGE ROHRER

BENEFIC PRESS · CHICAGO

The Moonbeam Books

MOONBEAM

MOONBEAM IS CAUGHT

MOONBEAM AND THE CAPTAIN

MOONBEAM AT THE ROCKET PORT

MOONBEAM AND THE ROCKET RIDE

MOONBEAM AND DAN STARR

MOONBEAM FINDS A MOON STONE

MOONBEAM AND SUNNY

MOONBEAM AND THE BIG JUMP

MOONBEAM IS LOST

Library of Congress
Number 67-17423

CONTENTS

The Moonworm

"Looks like rain," said Dr. Jim.

"Heeeen!" said Moonbeam.

The little space chimp was riding in a jeep with her friend Dr. Jim. They were riding fast, and Moonbeam liked that. She did not want it to rain. Rain would be no fun at all in an open jeep.

"Heeen!" Moonbeam said again.

Dr. Jim laughed.

"It will not rain for long, Moonbeam," he said. "The rains come and go very fast here at the Rocket Port."

After a time, a little rain fell.

"Heeen!" said Moonbeam.

More and more rain came down. Some fell on Moonbeam. Splat!

"Heeeen! Heeeen!" said Moonbeam.

Dr. Jim stopped the jeep.

"Come on, Moonbeam!" he called out. "Let's go in there!"

Moonbeam and Dr. Jim ran. Moonbeam ran so fast she did not know where she was going.

All at once Moonbeam was out of the rain. She looked around. She was in a very big house made up of one big room. It looked like the moon to her. But how could that be?

"Hon, hon!" she said.

Dr. Jim laughed.

"We call this the Moon House," he said. "It is just like the moon in many ways. When we want to know how something will work on the moon, we try it out in here."

Something was coming. Moonbeam looked up. When she saw it, she had to laugh. It was long and looked like a big worm.

"Hon, hon, hoon, hon," laughed Moonbeam.

"That must be the new Moonworm," said Dr. Jim. "The men are trying it out. On the moon, people will ride in it. And they will also use it to carry things."

Just then the Moonworm came to a stop. A door on it opened, and two men climbed out.

"They are heading our way," said Dr. Jim.

When one of the two men saw Dr. Jim and Moonbeam, he called out, "Dr. Jim!"

"That's Rocky Powers," said Dr. Jim to Moonbeam. "He is an astronaut like your friend Dan Starr. Rocky and Dan have been on many space trips together."

"Hoon! Hoon!" said Moonbeam. Moonbeam liked going on space trips. She would have liked to ride in space all the time.

Rocky Powers came up to talk to the little space chimp.

"You must be Moonbeam," he said. Then he turned to the other man. "Moonbeam has been to the moon, Mr. Brill," he said. "She is our one and only moon chimp."

"I am happy to know you, Moonbeam," said Mr. Brill.

"Mr. Brill is the man who has built the new Moonworm," Rocky said to Dr. Jim.

"How is the Moonworm doing on earth?" asked Dr. Jim.

"It works very well down here," said Mr. Brill. "In a few days, Rocky and I will lift off for the moon. The Moonworm will go up in another rocket. Then we will try it out on the moon."

"It is too bad you can't come with us, Moonbeam," said Rocky Powers. "A moon chimp like you would be a big help."

"Yes," said Mr. Brill. "Too bad."

"Heeeen!" said Moonbeam. She wanted to go. The three men laughed.

"You will get to the moon again soon," said Dr. Jim. "Just you wait and see!"

Moonbeam looked happier.

"Well, it's time for us to go back to the Moonworm," said Mr. Brill.

"See you soon, Moonbeam," said Rocky.

Dr. Jim turned to talk to Moonbeam.

"The rain must have stopped by now," he said. "Let's go out and see. If it has stopped, we will go and get Scott."

Dr. Jim was right. The rain had stopped. Moonbeam jumped into the jeep. Dr. Jim jumped in right after her.

"I will have to drive fast," he said, "to make up for lost time. Scott will be waiting."

"Hoon! Hoon!" said Moonbeam. Scott worked with Moonbeam at the Rocket Port, and she liked him. They were good friends.

The jeep soon was on its way again.

"Scott and I have a surprise for you," Dr. Jim said to Moonbeam.

"Hoon! Hoon!" said little Moonbeam.

Then Dr. Jim slowed down the jeep.

"There's Scott now," he said. He stopped the jeep for Scott. Scott jumped on. And Moonbeam jumped on Scott. Scott laughed.

"Where have you been, you two?" he said. "I have been waiting a long time."

"We ran in out of the rain," said Dr. Jim. "And we had a look at the Moonworm."

Dr. Jim started the jeep again. Soon it was on its way into town.

Scott turned to Moonbeam.

"So, you saw the Moonworm," he said.

"Hon, hon, hoon!" said Moonbeam.

"I hope it works well on the moon," said Scott. "It will soon be time to build the new lab up there. The men must have the help of the Moonworm for that."

"Where will the lab be built?" Dr. Jim wanted to know.

"The lab will be right on top of Mount X," said Scott. "It's a very high mountain. You can see a lot of the moon from its top."

The jeep was in town now, and Dr. Jim slowed it down. Moonbeam saw many people around her going into a big tent.

"That's where we are heading, too," said Dr. Jim. "That's where the surprise is."

"Hoon!" said Moonbeam. "Hoon! Hoon!"

Chimp on a Rope

The two men went into the tent with the little chimp. Moonbeam looked this way and that. All around the tent were people, people and more people.

Moonbeam did not know what to make of it, so she waited. Scott and Dr. Jim waited, too. So did all the other people. Then all at once the lights went out, and other lights went on. A man came out.

"And now," he called out, "here comes
Sunny, the Go-Go Chimp! You will see him
climb! You will see him jump and turn! And
you will see him walk on a rope high over your
heads! Here he comes now!"

Moonbeam looked. Then out into the light
came a chimp just like her!

"There's Sunny!" people called out.

"Ung! Ung!" said Sunny.

"Ung, ung?" said Moonbeam. "Hoon! Hoon!"

Then Sunny ran to a rope. Up and up he climbed. He jumped from one rope to another. He climbed on, and again he jumped.

"Look at that chimp go!" people called out.

When Sunny was high over their heads, he stopped climbing. Tied from one tower to another was a long, long rope.

Sunny looked at the long rope. Then slowly he walked out on it!

"Wow!" said a man. "Go, go, Sunny!"

All the people were looking up. Little by little Sunny made his way on the rope. Little by little he walked the rope from one tower to the other. Then there he was! He was on the other tower!

"He made it!" people called out.

"What a chimp!" said others.

Moonbeam did not know what to make of it all. She liked to have people look at her. After all, she was a space chimp! But now people were looking only at this other chimp. Moonbeam did not like that.

Sunny's rope walks and climbs came to an end. As he climbed down, the people called to him. "Good chimp, Sunny! Good work!"

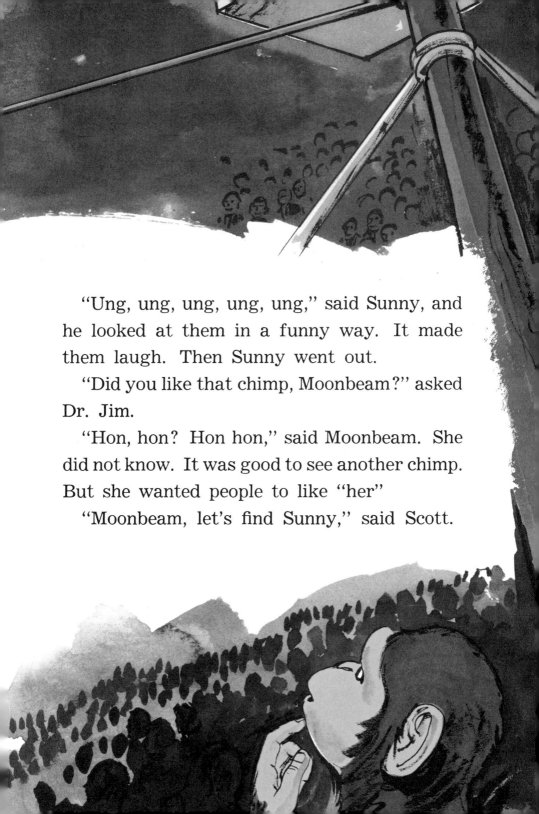

"Ung, ung, ung, ung, ung," said Sunny, and he looked at them in a funny way. It made them laugh. Then Sunny went out.

"Did you like that chimp, Moonbeam?" asked Dr. Jim.

"Hon, hon? Hon hon," said Moonbeam. She did not know. It was good to see another chimp. But she wanted people to like "her"

"Moonbeam, let's find Sunny," said Scott.

Moonbeam went with the two men. They found Sunny in a little room.

"Moonbeam," said Scott. "This is Sunny. Sunny, this is Moonbeam."

The two chimps looked at one another.

"Ung! Ung!" said Sunny. He looked happy to see Moonbeam.

"Hon, hon, hon," said Moonbeam.

Then Dr. Jim turned to her.

"And now comes the big surprise," he said. "Sunny is coming back to the Rocket Port with us. He is going to be a space chimp too."

Moonbeam looked at Dr. Jim. She looked at Sunny.

Dr. Jim went on, "With your help, Sunny can be a good space chimp. Then you and he can go on space trips together. What do you say to that, Moonbeam?"

"Heeeeeen!" was what Moonbeam said. "Heen!"

Now it was the men's turn to be surprised. They wanted the surprise to make her happy. But Moonbeam was not happy at all.

"What's this?" said Dr. Jim.

"Don't you want a friend with you on space trips?" said Scott.

"Heeen! Heeen!" said Moonbeam.

The two men looked at the two chimps. Then Dr. Jim turned to Scott.

"Now I get it!" he said. "Moonbeam likes being the only chimp at the Rocket Port! She wants to go on being the only space chimp."

"Well, that's too bad," said Scott. "It can't be helped, Moonbeam."

"Yes, Moonbeam," said Dr. Jim. "We must have two space chimps to help build the new lab on the moon."

21

"Heeeeen!" said Moonbeam.

It was time to get back to the Rocket Port.

"Come on, you two!" said Scott. "Let's go!"

"Sunny has a lot to learn," said Dr. Jim. "He must get a good start tomorrow."

Sunny jumped into the jeep. Moonbeam jumped in, too, but as far away from Sunny as she could get. Dr. Jim started the jeep.

Sunny did not know what to make of little Moonbeam. He liked the space chimp and wanted to be her friend. But every time he tried to get near her in the jeep, she moved away.

"Heen!" she said. "Heen! Heen!"

Sunny was good at jumping and rope walking. But he was not very good at making friends with another chimp! He moved near Moonbeam. She moved away. He jumped. She jumped away!

Scott did not want to laugh, but he could not help it. Soon Dr. Jim was laughing, too. The two chimps did not like it. By the time the jeep got back to the Rocket Port, they were doing nothing and saying nothing.

No Help From Moonbeam

The next day Scott called to Moonbeam. "Come on, let's go find Sunny."

But Moonbeam said nothing at all.

"You are a good space chimp," said Scott. "You can be a big help to Sunny."

Moonbeam came with Scott, but she did not look happy about it. They found Sunny going around on a ride.

"Sunny is learning about rocket rides," Scott told Moonbeam.

Soon the ride stopped. But Sunny did not stop. He went right on turning and turning.

"Look out!" said a man.

But it did no good. Sunny ran right into Dr. Jim! He fell, got up, and ran right into Scott. Only then did he come to a stop.

Moonbeam laughed and laughed.

"Ung, unnngg!" said Sunny, not very happy.

"Hon, hoon, hon, hon," laughed Moobeam.

"That's no way to help, Moonbeam," said Scott. "You could show Sunny the right way to ride a rocket."

But Moonbeam would do nothing to help Sunny. She only laughed and laughed at him.

And so it went all day. Sunny tried as well as he could. But learning to be a space chimp was very hard work. And Moonbeam did nothing to help him. Sunny did not do well.

Scott and Dr. Jim looked at Moonbeam.

"I didn't think she would be like this," said Scott. "Why won't she help Sunny?"

"With no help from Moonbeam, it will take Sunny a long time to learn," said Dr. Jim.

"But what can we do about it?" said Scott.

The two men did not know.

The days went by. Sunny did learn a little about rockets and space but much too slowly. Moonbeam did nothing but look on and laugh.

"It's time for Sunny to learn parachute jumping," said Dr. Jim one day.

"Do you think we can get Moonbeam to help him this time?" said Scott.

"Moonbeam can go up with Sunny," said Dr. Jim. "The two chimps can jump together. That may help Sunny to learn."

"Well, we can try it," said Scott. "It just may work."

Dr. Jim looked at Moonbeam.

"Time to go for a plane ride," he said.

"Hoon! Hoon!" said Moonbeam. She ran out and jumped into the jeep. When Moonbeam heard "ride," she wanted to get started soon. The two men got into the jeep after her, and they were soon on their way.

Sunny and a man were waiting at the plane. "Ung! Ung!" said Sunny to Moonbeam. He still wanted to be her friend. But Moonbeam said nothing and did not go near him. She did not want to be his friend at all.

The two chimps were soon on the plane. With them came Scott and the other man. Dr. Jim did not get on. He would stay at the Rocket Port and wait for Moonbeam and Sunny to parachute down.

Soon the plane started. On and on it went, and then, up from the Rocket Port it climbed. For a time, it went on climbing. Then Scott called out.

"That's it! The chimps can jump from here," said Scott.

The plane stopped climbing, and the man with Scott opened a door.

"Look at the Rocket Port!" he said. "How far down it is!"

Scott looked down.

"That's where you must jump to," he said to Sunny. "See?" Sunny looked down.

Sunny did not like the looks of it at all. He was a good rope climber. But there was no rope to climb on down there!

"Unnnnng, unnnng," he said.

"Hon, hon, hon," laughed Moonbeam.

Sunny did not want to jump. But then he did not like having Moonbeam laugh at him. So out the door he came!

"Good work Sunny!" said Scott. "Now it's your turn, Moonbeam."

Moonbeam had made many jumps. Out she came right after Sunny.

The chimps fell very fast at first. Then, one after another, their parachutes opened. That slowed them down.

"Hoon! Hoon!" said Moonbeam.

"Ung! Ung!" said Sunny. He liked this long ride down now. A parachute was just as good as a rope.

Down, down, down came the two chimps. It looked as if little by little the Rocket Port was coming to them! But Sunny did not see that. He was looking up at Moonbeam. He did not see where he was going.

Moonbeam saw. She saw that Sunny was heading right for a big tree! Moonbeam could have helped Sunny now. She could have said, "Heen! Heen!" Then Sunny would have looked down and jumped away from the tree. But Moonbeam did not want to help Sunny. So she said nothing.

Dr. Jim saw Sunny, too. He started to run. "Look out, Sunny!" he called. "Look out for that tree!"

But he was still too far away. Sunny could not hear him. The chimp went right on coming down and looking up. Then—crash! crackle! crunch! Sunny hit the tree.

"Ung, ung, ung, ung, ung!" said Sunny.

"Oh-oh!" said Dr. Jim.

"Hon, hon, hon," laughed Moonbeam. "Hon, hon, hoon, hon, hon."

When Dr. Jim came to the tree, he stopped and looked up at Sunny.

"Jump, Sunny," he called. "I know it's a big jump, but it's not too big for you."

Sunny tried to jump, but he could not do it. He was still tied into his parachute, and the parachute was all tied up in the tree!

"See if you can get out of your parachute," Dr. Jim called.

Sunny did not know what Dr. Jim wanted him to do. Again and again he tried to jump. Again and again the parachute stopped him.

The plane with Scott in it came back down to the Rocket Port, and Scott was soon at the tree, too. He did not like what he saw.

"Come on, Moonbeam," he said. "Help Sunny get down."

"Hon, hoon, hon, hon," laughed Moonbeam.

"If Sunny is not down soon," said Scott, "we will not be in time to see Rocky Powers and Mr. Brill lift off for the moon."

Moonbeam stopped laughing. She looked at Scott. Then she started to climb the tree. When she got to Sunny, she started to work on his parachute.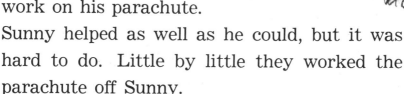
Sunny helped as well as he could, but it was hard to do. Little by little they worked the parachute off Sunny.

"Good work, you two!" called Scott.

"See what you two can do when you work together?" called Dr. Jim.

The two chimps looked at one another.

"Come on," called Scott. "The rockets will be lifting off."

Moonbeam and Sunny climbed down fast. They jumped into the jeep, and Dr. Jim started it up. Away they went riding fast.

"We will be there soon now," said Scott.

But Sunny had been up in the tree too long. They were still riding on their way when the time came for the rockets to lift off.

"Look!" said Scott.

Dr. Jim stopped the jeep fast, and they all jumped out to get a good look. Not far away it looked as if a big light went on. Then they could hear it, too. It was like many, many planes going by at one time. And then there it was! They saw the rocket slowly lifting up and away.

"Ung!" said Sunny. "Ung! Ung!"

"There go Rocky and Mr. Brill," said Scott.

Faster and faster went the big rocket. Another light went on, and then the other rocket came up.

"The Moonworm is in that one," said Scott.

"Hoon! Hoon!" said Moonbeam.

The two men and the two chimps looked after the two rockets for a long time. Then Dr. Jim looked down at Moonbeam.

"You like space rides, don't you?" he said. "You want to be a good space chimp and go on many space rides, right?"

"Hoon! Hoon!" said Moonbeam.

"Well, to be a good space chimp, you must help Sunny," said Dr. Jim. "We must have two good space chimps to help us build the new lab on the moon."

Moonbeam looked at him. She looked at Sunny. Slowly, she went up to Sunny.

"Hon, hon?" she said.

Sunny was happy. It looked as if Moonbeam wanted to be his friend after all. It made him want to jump! With a big "ung, ung!" he jumped up on the jeep, then up on Dr. Jim, then to Scott, then back on the jeep again. The two men laughed.

"You are making Sunny a very happy chimp, Moonbeam!" said Scott.

Just then, Sunny jumped back down again. He was moving so fast, he could not see where he was going. Down he came, right on top of little Moonbeam!

"Heeeeeeeeeeen!" said Moonbeam.

She got up and ran away from Sunny. Soon she stopped, but she would not look at him.

"Ung, ung?" said Sunny.

Moonbeam turned back. But when Sunny moved her way, she moved away from him. She would have nothing to do with a chimp that jumped on her.

Scott looked at Dr. Jim.

"We are back where we started," he said.

No one was happy about it.

Trouble on the Moon

After that, Moonbeam stayed away from Sunny. She did not laugh at him, but she did nothing to help him.

Still, Sunny was learning to be a space chimp. He would have learned faster with Moonbeam's help, but she did not give it.

"Well, there's nothing we can do about it," said Dr. Jim to Scott.

But then all at once Sunny did catch on! Soon he was learning very fast.

He learned how to go around and around and not run into people.

He learned to stay away from trees.

He learned to jump from a plane.

He learned how to get out of a parachute.

Scott and Dr. Jim were happy. Sunny was very happy. Only Moonbeam was not happy. She just looked on and said nothing.

One day Scott and Dr. Jim were watching Sunny work out on a long rope. They saw something coming at them very fast. Soon they saw that it was a jeep.

"That looks like trouble!" said Dr. Jim.

And trouble it was. The jeep came to stop, and the man driving it jumped out.

"General Winters wants you two," he said to Scott and Dr. Jim. "The chimps, too. Come on, let's go!"

"What's up?" said Scott.

"I don't know," said the man. "There is some trouble on the moon, I think."

Scott and Dr. Jim looked at one another.

"Rocky Powers!" said Scott.

"And Mr. Brill!" said Dr. Jim. He started running for his jeep. "Let's go find out!"

They found General Winters. With him was their astronaut friend, Dan Starr.

Moonbeam jumped into Dan's arms.

"Hoon! hoon!" she said.

General Winters looked at her.

"This is no time for fun, chimp," he said. "There's trouble on the moon."

"Rocky Powers and Mr. Brill have crashed into Mount X," said Dan Starr.

"Crashed on the moon!" said Scott. "Are they all right?"

"We don't know," said General Winters. "We have tried and tried to call them. But nothing comes back."

"What made them crash?" Dr. Jim asked.

"They were looking at Mount X to see where the new lab could be built," said General Winters. "They had just called us to tell us what they saw. Then all at once we heard nothing. I think their rocket must have come too close to the big mountain, and that's how it crashed."

"Can we do something to help Rocky and Mr. Brill?" Scott wanted to know.

"That's what I called you here for," said General Winters. "Dan Starr will lift off for the moon just as soon as we can get a rocket ready. Will the new space chimp be ready to go with him?"

"Two good space chimps could be a big help," said Dan Starr. "We may have to do a lot of climbing to find the lost men."

Dr. Jim and Scott looked at Sunny.

"Sunny still has much to learn," said Dr. Jim. "But he is doing very well. He can help."

"Good!" said General Winters. "Then Scott and the two chimps will go with Dan. Now go and get ready. See you at the rocket!"

General Winters went out. Dan Starr went soon after.

"Come on, Moonbeam! Come on, Sunny!" said Dr. Jim. "We will have to give you two a good looking over."

Dr. Jim started off fast with the two chimps. Scott went another way.

"You go on with them," he called after Dr. Jim. "I will go get our space suits."

Moonbeam, Sunny, and Dr. Jim moved fast. They were soon in a big room. It was the room where astronauts get ready for space trips. Many people inside were working fast.

In one part of the room was Dan Starr. All the men worked to get him ready.

Dr. Jim went to work on Moonbeam and Sunny. He worked fast, but he gave them a good looking over.

"On a space ride, every part of you must be working just right," said Dr. Jim. "If it didn't, you could be in trouble."

When Dr. Jim was working on Moonbeam, Scott came in with the space suits.

"Here are the two chimp suits," said Scott. Then with his own suit he went to get ready, too. They all wanted to get the rocket on its way as soon as they could. The men on the moon must have help fast.

Then Dr. Jim said, "You two look all right to me. Now let's put your space suits on!"

"Ready, chimps?" Dan Starr called.

"Ready!" Dr. Jim called back.

"Scott!" called Dan. "Ready?"

"Ready!" came Scott's voice.

"Good!" called Dan. "Let's get to that rocket ship."

Space Rock

General Winters was waiting at the rocket. The jeep soon came with Dan Starr, Scott, Moonbeam, and Sunny. The two men and the two chimps jumped out and walked over to General Winters. The General now took only one long look at them. Then he said, "Get up there! Find our men! Bring them back!"

Working men were moving away from the big rocket. One of the men came up to Dan.

"The rocket is ready to go," he said. "I hope you get there in time."

"I hope so, too," said Dan. He turned to Scott and the chimps. "Come on!" he said. "We have to hurry!"

The two men and the two chimps turned and headed for the rocket. They were soon riding up to the spaceship on top. General Winters saw them get in. Then the door of the big spaceship closed.

No one was working on the rocket now. No one was doing a thing. Everyone was looking at the big rocket and waiting. The time for lift-off came near.

"Three. . .two. . .one . . .LIFT-OFF!"

All at once a big light came on under the rocket. There was so much light that General Winters and the others had to turn their heads away. Then they could hear the rocket, too. It was as if the Rocket Port was moving under them. And then slowly the big rocket with its spaceship on top pushed off.

It started slowly, then went faster. Up, up, it came from the Rocket Port. General Winters looked after the big rocket. Soon he could see it no more.

"A good start!" he said. "I only hope they get there in time to help Rocky and Mr. Brill."

Higher and higher the rocket pushed from the Rocket Port. Inside the spaceship, Sunny tried to move. He could not do it.

"Unnnnnnnnnng!" he said.

"You will have to stay still for a time," Scott said to him.

"The rocket is giving us a big push just now," said Dan Starr. "The more the rocket pushes, the harder it is for us to move."

"Unnnng," said Sunny. He wanted to move.

"Soon the rocket's push will not be so hard," said Dan. "Then you can move around."

Moonbeam said nothing. She did not want to help Sunny get used to space.

For a time the rocket went on pushing the spaceship. That made it go faster and faster. Then Dan Starr looked at Scott.

"This is it!" he said. "This is as fast as we have to go."

The big rocket stopped pushing. A part of it came away from the spaceship.

Now Sunny had no trouble at all moving. That made him much happier.

"Ung! Ung!" he said.

Dan and Scott laughed. Moonbeam did not laugh. She turned her back on Sunny and the two men and looked out into space.

On and on went the spaceship, on its way to the moon. A day went by. Another day came. The moon looked nearer and nearer. Sunny was getting used to riding in space, too. He liked this trip. But Moonbeam did not.

"Just look at that chimp!" said Scott. "All she will do is look into space."

"If only she would be Sunny's friend," said Dan. "The chimps would be much more help on the moon if they could work well together."

"They may not be friends," said Scott, "but they will do all they can to help us. How about it, Sunny and Moonbeam?"

"Ung-ung!" said Sunny.

But Moonbeam was not looking at Scott. She was looking at something in space. She saw something coming right at them!

"Heen! Heen!" she called out. "Heeeeen!"
The men looked out.

"It's a space rock!" said Dan Starr. "A big
one, and its heading right for the ship!"

"It's coming fast!" said Scott. "Look out!"

There was no time to turn the ship, no time
to do a thing! The two men could only look
at the big rock come. Moonbeam didn't know
what way to turn. With a "Heen! Heen! Heen!"
she jumped over to Sunny and into his arms,
as if he could help her!

But the space rock did not crash into the ship. It came head on and then went by! Soon it was so far away that they could not see it anymore.

"Wow!" said Scott. "That was a close one!"

Dan was looking at Moonbeam and laughing. Moonbeam was still in Sunny's arms.

"That rock must have looked like the end to Moonbeam!" said Dan.

Moonbeam looked at the two men. Again people were laughing at her! She looked at Sunny. Every time she got near this chimp, something bad came of it! She jumped away from Sunny. She was looking into space again.

Another day came and went, and now the moon was very near.

"We will soon be ready to come down on it," said Dan Starr.

"What will we do then?" Scott asked. "How will we help Rocky and Mr. Brill?"

"We can't look for them with this spaceship," said Dan. "If we take it near Mount X, we may crash too."

"How will we find them?" Scott asked.

"We must find the Moonworm," said Dan. "It will take us to Mount X."

"If it works on the moon," said Scott.

"We must make it work," said Dan.

The two men said nothing more. It was time to come down to the moon.

On the Moon

Dan did something to the spaceship. It made the ship turn around. Now its head was turned away from the moon, and the men and chimps could not see it. Then slowly the spaceship came down, back end first.

"Get ready now," said Dan. "The ship's about to hit the moon."

They did not have long to wait. All at once the ship jumped a few times under them. Then it came to a stop on the moon.

"Good trip!" said Dan. He opened the door of the ship. "Now let's find that Moonworm!"

Dan, Scott, Moonbeam, and Sunny climbed down from their ship. On all sides of them the rocks of the moon gave off a hard, white light. It was something to see! But the men and chimps had little time to look around.

"The sooner we find the Moonworm," said Scott, "the more hope we have of finding the lost men in time."

They started to move away from one another and look around. Here and there, up and down they looked. Soon they could not see one another anymore.

Then all at once Sunny's voice came to the others from somewhere.

"Ung! Ung!" it said. "Ung! Ung!"

"What is that chimp doing?" said Dan Starr.

"Be still, Sunny!" Scott called to him. "We have work to do!"

"Unnnnnng! Ung, ung!" said Sunny.

"We will have to go after him, Dan," called Scott. "Let's go!"

They found Sunny jumping up and down on top of a big moon rock.

"Hon, hon, hoon, hon, hon, hon," laughed Moonbeam when she saw him.

"Come down from there!" called Scott. "This is no time to be a funny chimp!"

"Wait!" said Dan. "I think he is looking at something on the other side of the rock!"

The two men and Moonbeam all climbed after Sunny and looked down. On the other side of the rock was the Moonworm!

"He has found it!" said Scott.

"Good work, Sunny!" said Dan. "What a good chimp you are!"

Moonbeam stopped laughing. That other chimp again! Moonbeam wanted the men to tell her that she was a good chimp. But no! They were telling that to Sunny. Moonbeam walked slowly to the Moonworm with Sunny and the men. She was not happy at all.

They climbed into the Moonworm. Dan tried to start it. It did not start.

"Try again," said Scott.

Dan tried again. This time it started.

"So far, so good," said Dan. "Now let's see how it runs here on the moon."

At first, the Moonworm did not run right. It jumped this way and that and would not head the right way.

"I may not be doing it right," said Dan. "Let me try it another way."

Dan worked and worked at it. Then all at once the Moonworm was off and away!

"You have it now!" said Scott. "That's the way to drive it."

"It's running well now," said Dan. "On to Mount X!"

On and on went the Moonworm. Dan did the driving. The others looked around them at the still, white moon rocks.

"Look!" said Scott. "There are the big mountains!"

"How high they are!" said Dan.

"Can you see Mount X?" asked Scott.

55

"Not from here," said Dan. "First we must climb high up. Only then will we see it."

As soon as the Moonworm started to climb into the mountains, it slowed down. The more the Moonworm had to climb, the slower it went.

"Looks like more work for Mr. Brill," said Dan Starr.

"Yes," said Scott. "He will have to make a good climber out of this worm."

But the men were not happy. "Yes," they were thinking, "Mr. Brill will do it, if we get to him in time."

Higher and higher climbed the Moonworm. Slower and slower it moved. They could see far down now. Still the Moonworm climbed. But the way up was getting harder and harder. Then all at once Dan stopped the Moonworm.

"What's up?" said Scott.

"Look at where we have to go," said Dan. "Do you think the Moonworm can make it?"

Scott looked where Dan was looking.

"I don't know," he said. "We could go back and try another way."

"There's no time," said Dan. "We must get to Mount X fast. And this Moonworm is getting slower all the time."

"We must try it this way then," said Scott. "I am ready if you are."

Dan started the Moonworm up again. Slowly it climbed, slowly. Then it stopped. It was too much of a climb. It could go no more.

Up and Up

"Heeeeeeen!" said Moonbeam.

"Well, now what, Dan?" said Scott.

"The Moonworm will have to stay here," said Dan. "From now on, we are on our own."

"If the Moonworm could not climb it, how can we?" said Scott. "I know that I am not a good mountain climber."

"We are very light on the moon," said Dan. "At the Rocket Port we could not climb like this. Here it will not be so hard."

Scott did not like the looks of it. But he was ready to try.

"We just can't give up now," he said.

From inside the Moonworm the men picked some things. They took a tent, some long ropes, things to eat, and things to help them climb. Each man and chimp carried something on his back. Then the big climb was on again.

It was slow going. Little by little they made their way higher and higher. For the chimps the climb was no trouble at all.

For the astronauts it was a hard, hard climb. The more they climbed, the harder it got. But they did not give up. On and on they climbed on the moon.

But the time came when they could climb no more.

"That's all," said Scott, and stopped. "I can't make another move."

Dan stopped climbing, too.

"Yes," he said. "I was about ready to fall down, too."

For a time, the two men just stayed there saying nothing. The chimps didn't know what to make of it. Then Scott turned to Dan.

"What now, Dan?" he said. "What now?"

"Let's put up the tent," said Dan. "Inside we will be out of the light. Then we can get some sleep."

"Yes," said Scott. "After a little sleep, it will not be so hard to climb."

"Right," said Dan. "But we must not sleep too long. We must get on to Mount X."

"How far is it now?" asked Scott, as he helped Dan put up the tent.

"I don't know," said Dan. "But I don't think we have far to go."

"Good," said Scott. When the tent was up, he went inside. He started to think about the two lost men again. But then little by little he went to sleep. Soon they were all sleeping.

When they got up again, Scott tried moving around a little.

"That was good," he said. "I think that little sleep was a big help."

Scott was right. When they started on their way again, they found that the climbing was not so hard for them. On and on, higher and higher the two men and two chimps climbed.

"Where is that Mount X?" said Dan Starr. "We have climbed high into the mountains, and still no Mount X!"

But just then they heard Moonbeam say, "Hoon! Hon, hon, hoon!"

Sunny and the two men looked up, and there they saw a mountain like no other mountain.

"That's it!" said Dan. "That's Mount X. What a mountain!"

"It's just right for the new lab," said Scott. "How high it is!"

As they looked up at Mount X, something came into Scott's head.

"But where is the crashed spaceship?" he said. "I can't see any spaceship!"

Dan looked and looked at the mountain, but he could not see a spaceship.

"It may be on the other side," he said. "We must climb up and look for it."

And so the climb started all over again.

They were soon climbing right up Mount X. It was hard, slow going. And it got harder. Many big rocks were in the way. They could climb over some of them. They had to go around others. At times, they had to jump from rock to rock. The long climb went on.

"Where can that spaceship be?" said Scott after a time.

"We will be to the top of Mount X soon," said Dan. "I am starting to think the lost spaceship is not here at all."

He did not look happy about it.

"Well, we can't stop now," said Scott, and he went on climbing.

Dan and the chimps looked at Scott's back. Then they started after him. When they had climbed around some rocks not far from the mountain's top, Dan came to a stop.

"Scott!" he called. "Look! Up there!" At the side of the big mountain was a high tower of rock. It looked high and hard and white in the moon's light. And there, right at its top, was the crashed rocket ship!

Climb, Moonbeam

"Ung! Ung!" said Sunny.

"Hoon! Hoon!" said Moonbeam.

"There it is!" said Scott.

"It's the ship, all right!" said Dan.

For a time, the two men and two chimps just looked at the crashed ship. They could see nothing at all was moving up there!

"Uh-oh!" Scott said. "I don't see Rocky or Mr. Brill!"

"That's right!" said Dan.

"Let's hope the two of them are still alive," said Scott.

"Well, there's only one way to find out," said Dan. "We must climb up there."

"But how?" Scott wanted to know.

Dan looked hard at the tower. Then the two of them looked all around it, but they could find no way up to the top.

"No man can climb that thing!" said Dan. The two men looked at one another. They did not know what to do.

"After all that work," said Dan. "Is this the end of the trip, and the two men?"

"No man can climb up there," Scott said. "But a chimp can! After all, what did we bring the chimps with us for?"

"That's it!" said Dan Starr. "One of the chimps can climb up and bring a long rope to the top."

"Right!" said Scott. "When one end of the rope is tied to the top of the rock, the chimp can throw the other end back down. Then one of us can climb up the rope, and we can save the men."

The two men turned to look at Moonbeam. Then they looked at Sunny. The two chimps looked back at the men.

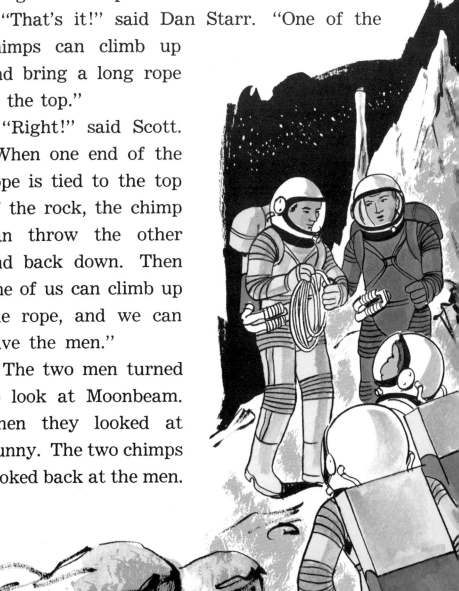

"Moonbeam, I think," said Scott. "Sunny is a good climber, but he has not been a space chimp for long. He may not be ready to do so much with no help from us."

Scott let Moonbeam know what he wanted her to do. "It's up to you, little Moonbeam!" he said.

Moonbeam was very happy. She would show that other chimp!

"Are you ready to go Moonbeam?" asked Scott. "Up you go."

Moonbeam was ready. She took one look at Sunny, as if to say, "Now you will see a good space chimp at work!" Then she started up the high rock tower.

But the tower was a surprise to Moonbeam. It was hard climbing. It was like no other climbing she had tried! Again and again she had to stop, come down a little way, and try another part of the tower.

"That's a hard climb," said Dan. "What if she can't make it?"

But Moonbeam would not give up. Again and again she tried to find a good way up. And then all at once she did find a way! Little by little she was climbing.

"That's it, Moonbeam!" called Dan Starr.

"Climb, Moonbeam! Climb!" called Scott.

"Ung! Ung!" called Sunny. He was happy for Moonbeam.

She was near the top when the climb all at once got hard again. Moonbeam had to slow down, then stop. She looked for a way to go on, but she could not find it.

"Uh-oh!" said Dan.

"Unnnnnnnnng!" said Sunny.

"Come on, Moonbeam!" Scott called to her. "You can do it!"

Moonbeam heard Scott and looked down at him. It nearly made her fall!

She took a big jump, then another one. All at once she looked around her. She was on top of the tower!

"She made it!" said Dan Starr.

Moonbeam looked at the rope she was carrying. Then she looked around for a big rock. Soon she found a part of the rock tower. She put one end of the rope around it. She let the other end fall down to the men.

Now it was Scott's turn to climb. Soon Scott was on his way up. Little by little he worked his way up the long rope.

"Hoon! Hoooon!" called Moonbeam.

But then there was more trouble.

"Look out for that big rock!" called Dan.

A big rock was in Scott's way. Scott stopped climbing and looked at it. Then he tried to work his way around it. He moved this way and that, but still the rock was in his way. Then all at once Moonbeam's voice came to him.

"Heeeeeeeeeeen!" it said.

Scott looked up and saw the big rock start to come away from the tower. Working fast, he moved over to one side. He got out of the way just in time. The big rock came crashing by very near him.

"We must look out for this tower," he called down to Dan Starr. "Its rocks are not as hard as they look. I hope they stay together."

Then Scott started climbing up the rope again. With the big rock out of the way, it did not take him long to get to the top.

"Hoon! Hoon!" said little Moonbeam.

"I am happy to see you, too," said Scott, laughing. But then he looked away from little Moonbeam and stopped laughing.

He was looking at the crashed spaceship. Moonbeam looked. She saw that all was still.

Help for the Lost Men

"Come on!" said Scott. "Let's have a look inside that ship!"

They tried the door of the spaceship, but it would not open at first. Then as Scott worked on it, it started to move.

What would they find inside? How would the two lost men be? What had stopped them from moving and from getting out of the ship?

Well, they would soon find out now. Scott soon had the door open. In no time at all, he and Moonbeam were inside the ship.

"There they are!" said Scott.

Rocky Powers lay there looking at them. He looked all right, but he could not move. A part of the rocket ship had come down on top of him. It stopped him from moving.

Mr. Brill lay at Rocky's side. From time to time, he moved his head or one of his arms. It was as if he could not see the others.

"Heen! Heen!" said Moonbeam.

"He is hurt," said Scott. "But I don't think it is too bad."

Then he turned back to Rocky. "Can you hear me, Rocky?" he called out.

Nothing came from Rocky.

Scott went to work on Rocky's space suit. He did something to it, and tried again.

"Rocky! Can you hear me?" said Scott.

And this time Rocky's voice came to them!

"I can hear you!" Rocky said. "Man! Am I happy to see you two!"

"Are you all right?" asked Scott.

"Yes, but I can't move," said Rocky. "It's this thing on top of me."

"Moonbeam and I will work on it," said Scott. "I think we can get it off you."

Scott and Moonbeam went to work.

"You can start by getting the climbing rope up here, Moonbeam," said Scott. "We can use it to help lift that thing away from Rocky."

Moonbeam did what Scott wanted. Scott took the rope end from her. He tied it to the part of the spaceship that lay on top of Rocky. The other end was still tied to the tower.

For a time, Scott worked with the rope, and Moonbeam looked on. Then he turned to her.

"I can use your help with the lifting now," he said. "Here, take this part of the rope."

Moonbeam took it from him.

"Now, ready. . .together. . .LIFT!" called out Scott

Nothing. Scott looked at the rope, then moved it a little.

"Again now. . .together. . .LIFT!" he called out to Moonbeam.

Moonbeam and Scott lifted hard.

"It's coming! I can tell!" said Rocky. "I can move a little now!"

"LIFT!" said Scott.

"Just a little more now!" said Rocky.

"Again. . .LIFT!" said Scott.

"That's it!" Rocky called out. "If only you can just make it stay there."

Slowly, Rocky worked his way. Then he was out from under.

"You can let go now, you two!" he said.

But when Scott and Moonbeam let go, trouble came. All at once the rock tower started to move under them! Dan Starr's voice came up.

"Look out! The tower is falling," he said.

The tower was moving, but it did not fall. It moved a little, then stopped.

"That was close!" said Scott. "If this tower falls, it's the end of us!"

"It moved just after we crashed," said Rocky. "Now all this climbing and lifting has made it move again. If it moves one more time, it could fall on us!"

"We will have to work slowly from now on," said Scott. "No jumping around, Moonbeam!"

Little by little the work went on. Rocky looked at Mr. Brill.

"He will be all right, I think," he said. "But we must find a way to get him down from here. We must get him back to the Rocket Port for help."

Scott looked at Mr. Brill. Then he looked at the long rope.

"The rope will help us," he said. "So will some parts of this big spaceship."

Scott picked up the rope and the parts. He started building.

"I learned how to make this from Dr. Jim," he said.

It was soon ready. Rocky helped Scott lift Mr. Brill, lay him down on it, and tie him to it. Then they tied Mr. Brill to Scott's back.

"Ready for the long climb down?" Scott asked Rocky.

"Ready!" said Rocky.

"Hoon! Hoon!" said Moonbeam. "Hoon!"

"You can go first, Rocky," said Scott. "I will come after you with Mr. Brill. Then Moonbeam can come."

Climbing down the rope was hard for Rocky. He had not moved in a long time. And he had not had a thing to eat in days. But slowly he worked his way down. Then down he was with Dan Starr. He was happy to see his good friend Dan again.

Now it was Scott's turn to use the rope with Mr. Brill tied to his back.

"Heen! Heen!" said Moonbeam when she saw him start down.

"It's all right, Moonbeam," laughed Scott. "Mr. Brill is very light here on the moon. It will be a hard climb, but I will make it."

Scott was right. He had to move slowly, but all went well. Scott and Mr. Brill had just made it down when a call came from Moonbeam.

"Heeeeeeeeeen!" she called out. "Heeeeeen!"

Scott, Dan, Rocky, and Sunny looked up fast. What they saw made them jump to one side just as fast as they could. The climb down had made the high rock tower move again.

A big part of the tower came crashing down, down! On every side of Sunny and the men, big and little rocks hit!

When it was over, the men looked at one another and at Sunny.

"Are any of you hurt?" Rocky asked.

"Nothing hit me," said Scott.

"I was not hurt," said Dan. "Sunny and Mr. Brill look all right."

Then Scott looked up.

"But what about Moonbeam?" he said. Then he called out, "Moonbeam. Where are you?"

At first, the men saw nothing at the top of the rock tower. Then little by little a head looked out over the side of the tower.

"Heeeeeeen! Heeeeeeen! Heeeeen!" a little voice said.

"Are you all right, Moonbeam?" Scott called. "Can you climb down from there?"

Moonbeam looked down.

"Heeeeeen!" she said. She did not move.

"Is she hurt?" asked Dan.

"I don't think so," said Scott. "But all this climbing and work and trouble have been too much for her. She can't do any more hard climbing on this trip."

"Then how can we get her down from there now?" Rocky wanted to know.

The others all looked at Rocky. Then they looked at the rock tower. No one could climb up it now—no man and no chimp.

For a long time no one said a thing.

Mount Moonbeam

Scott was thinking as hard as he could. He looked at Moonbeam, at the rock tower, at Sunny. Then he looked at the top of Mount X, and all at once something came to him!

"Sunny!" he said. "Sunny will do it!"

The others all turned to him. They looked at him as if he had lost his head.

"You know Sunny can't climb that tower now!" said Dan. "No chimp could!"

"Yes, I know," was all that Scott said.

"Then what are you up to?" Rocky wanted to know.

But Scott would tell them nothing more about it. He called to Moonbeam.

"Don't give up, Moonbeam! Sunny and I will get you down!" Scott said.

Things looked so bad to Moonbeam that "Heeeeen!" was all she could say.

Scott started looking around.

"Come on, men. Don't just look at each other!" he said. "Help me find that long rope! It fell down when the rocks crashed."

The others did not know what to make of Scott. But they did want to help him. They started looking for the rope.

"Here it is!" said Rocky. He picked it up. "Now, what do you want it for?"

"Wait and see!" was all Scott would say as he took the rope from Rocky. Then he turned to Sunny.

"Come on, Sunny!" he said. "Let's see if you can still do some of the things you used to do in that big tent!"

"Ung, ung?" said Sunny. He did not know what it was all about, but he was happy to go with Scott. He wanted to help Moonbeam, too.

Scott and Sunny started climbing. But they did not try to climb the rock tower. They were on their way up Mount X!

"Where are you going?" Rocky called after Scott. "That is not the right way!"

"Moonbeam is not on Mount X!" called Dan Starr. "Come back down!"

But Scott and Sunny did not look back. Little by little they climbed Mount X. Sunny would jump on and up a little way. Then he would stop and wait for Scott to catch up.

"Ung-ung?" he would say.

Scott thought, "Can this little chimp do it? Can he do what he must? And can I do my part? Well, we will soon see."

Scott and Sunny climbed and climbed. Slowly they moved up the mountain. The top was very near now. But Scott did not want to get to the top.

"Stop climbing, Sunny!" he said all at once. "Here we are."

Sunny stopped and looked around. Not far away was the big rock tower. They were just as high as its top now. Now Sunny could see Moonbeam very well. And Moonbeam looked back at them. The other men looked at them, too.

"What good will this do?" Rocky said.

"You can't jump to the tower from where you are, Scott," said Dan. "It's too far!"

But Scott was not thinking of jumping. He took the long rope and called to Moonbeam.

"Can you hear me, Moonbeam?" he asked.

"Hon, hon, hon?" said Moonbeam. She heard him now.

"Good!" said Scott. "I will throw one end of this rope over to you. You must try to catch it!"

"Hoon, hon, hon, heen," said Moonbeam. She was ready.

Scott lifted his arm back over his head. Then, as hard as he could, he let the rope go. Little Moonbeam saw it come. It came close, but it did not go all the way to the tower. Moonbeam could not catch it.

When Scott had all of the rope back, he was ready to try again.

"Ready, Moonbeam?" he called.

"Hon, hon," said Moonbeam.

Again Scott's arm went back. And again his hard throw went out. The rope came very close this time. Moonbeam tried to catch it and nearly fell off the tower!

"Heeeeen!" she said, and let the rope go.

"Look out, little chimp!" Scott called to her. "Let the rope come to you. Don't go after it!"

Scott gave it another try, and this time his throw was good. The rope went all the way to Moonbeam. All she had to do was lift one arm, and she had it.

"Good catch!" called Scott. "Now tie it around that big rock."

Moonbeam put the rope end around the rock. On his side, Scott tied the other end to a big rock on Mount X. Then he turned to Sunny. Sunny was looking at the rope.

"That's right, Sunny!" said Scott. "The rope is for you to walk on! Can you do it?"

"Ung! Ung!" said Sunny.

"Good!" said Scott. "Go over there and get our Moonbeam!"

Sunny took a long look at the rope. Then little by little he walked out on it. This was something he could do well. Slowly he moved on, making his way on the long rope.

"That's it, Sunny!" called Scott.

"Go, Sunny, go!"
came Dan Starr's voice.

Little by little Sunny
walked the rope over to
the tower. Moonbeam
was looking at Sunny
come to her. He is not
so bad a chimp after
all! Then there he was
on the tower with her!

"Hoon!" she said.

"Ung!" said Sunny.

"So far, so good,"
called Scott to them.
"But now comes the
hard part. You have
to carry Moonbeam
back here, Sunny."

"Ung," said Sunny.

"Now, Moonbeam,"
said Scott. "You climb
on his back and stay
as still as you can."

"Heen!" said Moonbeam. She did not know if this would work, but there was no other way. So, up on Sunny's back she climbed.

Slowly, very, very slowly Sunny walked the rope with Moonbeam on his back.

"Wow!" came Rocky Powers' voice.

"Shhh!" said Scott.

On and on Sunny walked. Then, trouble! A rock on the tower moved, and the long rope started to move from side to side! Sunny stopped walking.

"Stay very, very, still now, Moonbeam!"
Scott called out.

Moonbeam stayed still, but Sunny could not
help moving. He came very near to falling!

"Look out!" came Dan Starr's voice.

"Shhh!" said Scott. Little by little the rope
slowed down and stopped. Sunny started
walking again. And then he and Moonbeam
were on Mount X with Scott!

"What a chimp!" came Dan's voice.

"What a walk!" came Rocky's voice.

"Hoon! Hoon! Hoon! Hoon!" said Moonbeam.

Scott and the two chimps started climbing down to the others. And just then the end came for the big rock tower! Dan was looking up and saw it coming.

"Scott! Moonbeam! Sunny!" he called. "Get out of the way!"

The man and chimps got out of the way just in time. They saw the tower move this way and that. Then it fell into many parts, and they all came crashing down! Down, down the big rocks fell. When they stopped, the big tower was no more.

Scott and the chimps soon made their way
back to the others. They found that Mr. Brill
was getting up. Dan Starr and Rocky had
been working on him.

"Where am I?" he was saying. "What's
going on?"

"You will be all right again soon," said Dan
Starr. "Your spaceship crashed, and you were
hurt. You had a bad time of it."

"And if it had not been for Moonbeam's good work," said Rocky, "it would have been the end of us. We would be under those rocks down there now!"

"We must do something for Moonbeam," said Mr. Brill. He looked around. "But what?"

Rocky looked up at Mount X.

"I know!" he said. "Mount X is not a good name for that big mountain. We can call it after Moonbeam!"

"Mount Moonbeam?" said Dan. "That's very good! That's very, very good!"

MOUNT MOONBE

"Did you hear, Moonbeam?" said Scott. "All the people will say that it's your mountain. Mount Moonbeam!"

"Hoon!" said Moonbeam. "Hoon! Hoon!"

"Ung! Ung!" said Sunny. He was happy for her. Moonbeam went over to him.

"Hon?" she said. "Hon, hon?"

The others laughed and laughed. Then Scott turned to them.

"Well, men," he said. "Let's head back for the Moonworm!"

"And then back to our spaceship!" said Dan.

"And then back to the Rocket Port!" said Rocky Powers.

"And then back to General Winters," said Mr. Brill. "Do we have a lot to tell him!"

The men turned and headed down the big mountain. With them came the two chimps. Sunny and Moonbeam walked together. They were friends now.

VOCABULARY

The total vocabulary of this book is 262 words, excluding proper names and sound words. The 5 words in roman type should be familiar to children reading on a third-grade level. The 6 words above third-grade level are shown in italic type. The number indicates the page on which the word first appears.

astronaut 9	*lab* 13	*rocket* 6
chimp 5	own 42	*space* 5
crashed 39		
	parachute 27	
jeep 5	plane 27	tower 17